# Elephants And Grapes

To MAilene —

Best,

[signature]

2024

Tom Portz

# DEDICATION

For my mother,

**Mary Mulder Portz**

She was a humble woman of intelligence, kindness, and compassion.

I am her fortunate son, better for her counsel and care.

# TABLE OF CONTENTS

# Introduction

*"Three of four times, you've returned from a place few people ever come back from".* My doctor has a way of reducing things to simple words.

Skating on the edge of death and knowing that's the case amplifies the sense of the mind, body, and time. It's too easy to say that nothing should be taken for granted. It isn't a hollow notion that life must be lived today – lived for all it is worth. Tomorrow is coming, but not with certainty.

I had a good mother with many attributes. She encouraged me to try to understand people and things. Above all, speak! Not in loud prattle, but if one saw grace or conflict, consider it. Evaluate it. Come to conclusions. Express your feelings even more so about people. If someone has done something nice, say so. If a person is attractive – in form or soul - make an honest attempt to let them know. If love captures your heart, share that passion.

Often, I have written something to express my inner feelings. Early on, I may have felt more comfortable with words written rather than spoken. Words upon a tangible page seemed like a buffer. There was a difference between what was read and what I would have said – a measure of emotional safety. That need for safety is something I have long outgrown. Looking back, I have no regret for any thought written and any verse shared.

Many of the poems I wrote were to exceptional people in my life. It was the realization of death that prompted me to gather together some of those writings for publication. Better to memorialize them than have the kids toss boxes and boxes of notes, poems, and stuff in the trash.

My thoughts and feelings have now been recorded and shared. More will follow.

I have marveled at cheery flowers, crystal clear waters, and the majesty of the Moon. With darker reflection, my pains have been voiced. My being is grateful for the precious people who are, and will always be, a part of my life. Those souls are rare. They have captivated my mind.

I have told them how they stirred all that I am and how much I love them.

### Elephants and Grapes

I love you.

I love you so much –

     more than treasures captured or created,

     more than the giddy fever of first love

     or the intimate grace of an aged union,

     even more than the delicious adoration

     of elephants and grapes,

     a lot more.


I love you more than koala bears, baklava, and regal hotels -

     the kind with elegant perfume trays in the bathrooms,

     and shower chambers, where the water falls like rain.


More than mojitos, pale ale, and martinis with bleu cheese olives,

     but then I don't drink -

     they may not be the best measure.

I love you more than chilled shrimp with lemon and cocktail sauce,

more than watermelon pickles -

those wicked-good homemade sweet pickles that are good for the boy parts.


More than Ferris wheels, San Francisco, and hand-crafted tin roof gelato -

which is a truly decadent knock-off of a chocolate sundae with peanuts,


And even more than Diet Pepsi,

but I do pause a moment to think about Diet Pepsi.


I love you more than crisp, high-count, wind-washed sheets-

lavish down pillows,

and a few boy-girl things we could research together.


My head is a tingly swirl -

thinking, wishing, and hoping any number of things,

all good, and all sparking happily and painfully within me.

2

I am profoundly grateful that you love me too -

at least for our shared eternity.

# Broken

**I am broken in a way that has no fix.**

It is my sad regret,

for my limitations,

my scatter –

that which is torn and wrecked.

Not for surgery and sutures, grafts, or mending plates,

Not for wishes, hope, or prayers,

Not for time -yet another pain -

all the worse as it runs away

stealing those moments of life.


**I am broken in a way that has no fix.**

A clear mind dims.

Not for dementia, or demons, or ghosts,

Not for meds, wounds, or dressings,

Not for clutter, but for the pressure of working to live.

**I am broken in a way that has no fix.**

My pain exhausts me.

Not that I cannot endure, or try to,

Not that it is flaring, though it does,

Not as a surprise, for I am done and want it gone.


**I am broken in a way that has no fix.**

I am a speck on an organic ball near a small star.

Not that I feel large or grand,

Not that I feel alone, though I do,

Not that I am without comfort, for I think there is more.


**I am broken, and I accept what is beyond the fix.**

## The Large of My Day

The toaster was out.

So was the butter, a fresh quarter stick straddling that special dish – the one you bought.

And you set a hefty knife, a man-sized plate, and of course,

    a loaf of bread – urban edgy with nuts and seeds.

    Good though.

You got up before me.

You weren't being careless.

It was a string of markers, of duties.

Not for me. I needn't clean up.

It wasn't a message – well, actually it was.

You care about me.

You are kind and thoughtful, and all of those simple obvious phrases.

After your own pitifully small pass at breakfast,

you assemble and reassemble something for me –

something I will like.

I am aware – of you.

I am fortunate.

I am grateful.

You are the small and the large of my day.

How Loving.

## Waining Life

I am living but lifeless.

Life loops and loops,

And I go absolutely nowhere.


There is a nagging twang in my head,

whining that I am squandering time.

And I don't have time.


Those people, so many people.

They perceive my construction,

yet they do not know, nor should they.


I am sick,

but among my sicknesses

is an unbridled fury for those who say:

*You're Alive* or *Toughen Up.*


I am sad, oddly tired, and in pain.

This day and this night are null markers

in a wasting life.


I want more.

I need more –

a body rekindled by attendant divinity,

heartbeats that are clean and true,

a new burst of overwhelming optimism –

to move,

to succeed,

to truly heal,

to be wonderfully alive.


Talk won't matter,

it seems all my place to mend and regroup –

to attack the fragmented body beast.

But my head is too doggedly charged to rest.

I am beneath what makes people smile.

# In My Space

I wish you were in my space.

Too close for anyone, save someone you would share your envelope with.

So close that without touch, I could sense and feel you.

So close that there is a welcome panic.

So close that the natural moment begs you to be drawn still nearer.

So close that a kiss is expected, and effortless.

A hand mindlessly pulls you to me.

Tensions rise and fall, both happily evolving into an honest passion.

Without words, you are told that you are important, and cherished, and that you are truly loved.

In my space and at that time, there would be nothing between us.

## The Last Before Sleep

It is good – so good.

In body and mind, I am pointed toward you.

Though you are far, you are within me – completely within me.

Sympathetic and symmetric, I feel you.

And my heart is troubled – happily troubled.

All the day, and to the last before sleep, it is you.

Hope teases my soul as I am not there – but I will get there.

The whole of my body relishes you.

Time passes, and I am close – hours close.

I will hold your hands, and touch your face, and hips.

It is deep – inexplicably deep.

I love you in infinite magnitudes.

## Wildflowers

We call them wildflowers,
    But we'd rather they grow here or there.

We call them wildflowers,
    But we'd rather they were this height or that.

We call them wildflowers,
    But we'd rather they were yellow or blue.

We call them wildflowers,
    But we'd rather they bloom early or late.

We call them wildflowers,
    But they are now familiar, captive, even tamed.

# Love Should Bloom

You sparkle in the candlelight.

Eyes – always eyes.

Cheeks, soft but radiant in blushing pinks.

Hair – cascading drizzles that frame a face.

Your lips seem bigger, moist,
        wanting and welcoming, and present – to me.

There is so much more – feminine and loving,
        swirling with a sense of hope, of desire.

All, and the rest that is to be.

We need not speak.

Words should be quiet.

Love should bloom.

## The Dog's Tale

Lucky dog.

The world was noisy, even at seven years old.
Life had prickly moments, though most pale compared to
my modern older life.

But the dog's tail wagged and wagged.
Running, jumping, and then the long lounges – sleeping,
need not a stick to measure the happiness, the fun.

The dog – so much of a life lived with little or no requested
permission.

Better still,
spiffy and clean,
the little dog, the one with super soft hair,
had fingers of every age rubbing his chest and chin.

Those same people lavished bright smiles,
showering joy akin to the warmth of the Sun.

Made sense.
The dog was loved – really loved.
So too, at any hour of the day,
the dog loved me – unconditionally.

A sweet friend.
A sweet life – for him, but also for me.

It was –
at age seven, even a few more.
I wondered.

Sometimes I wished – that I could be a dog.

## Kiss Me Backward

Stand near me.
Face me – please.
Let me smile. Just let me smile.

No need to talk.
I can read your eyes.
Pretty eyes. I have always thought so.

How important you are - to me.
You always excite me.
I feel that halo of trust, of soulful affection.

A little closer.
I lean into you.
There is a commonality – warmth.

You are as you were.
You are as you will be.
At least as I see you, and feel you.

It is time to kiss.
Always special.
Nothing new, and always new.

But,
and this is woeful.
Deep sadness invades my soul.

Alone,
you are not here.
I am dancing in an illusion.

Return.
Come to me again.
Share a love that was, a love that is - endless.

You are my partner in all the cosmos.
Kiss me.
And kiss me again.

Kiss me backward.

# Genesis

Forth, from the nothing that was before,

> from the shapeless, the odorless,

> from the Ether sprang new - heat, light, and mass.

Born of that naked singularity was time,

> measuring existence then, and unto this eternity.

Came of nothing, was chaos, an irony,

> for chaos was in fact – order.

*And later, someone would call this Reality.*

Majesty, as energy ground, fluid carvings of chiseled lines – out.

Matter, a new thing, ran fast.

Tensor pull, fumes, motion begat twirls;

> all, at every instant, pierced Ether's rim.

As did that part of Ether die,

> so arrived at this - place.

*And later, someone would call this Space.*

The perfection of blackness became visibly flecked.

The observable shape would emerge.

Of the many, they were all violent – swirls,

17

crackling in flame and pressure.

Of the many, it would become the common path – fire.

*And later, someone would call them Stars.*

Unique, yet in any case,

This star - our Sun - did foster new conditions of dust, dirt, and rock.

One place – blue - veiled in diaphanous clouds,

would move dutiful, about its generous Sun.

*And later, someone would call this Planet, properly Earth.*

Perched distant from this sun, yet close in this infinity,

this planet would spark organic,

roots of green things clawed its hide.

Gathered liquids, spilling about

in topical veiny lines on the planet's skin.

Something came of nothing, then the reality,

of space, and start, and the planet.

*And later, someone would call this life.*
Stasis was not, Earth changed.

Of flora, muck, and goo,

did come beasts and creatures of thought.

They would live - there, on the Sun's son,

in a reality that the Ether alone was long gone.

Pondering at night, they watch the flecks as they toil.

They gaze, they marvel

in wonder at the spotted darkness.

*And later, they would be called Man.*

## The Eternal Scar

I can't love you less.

There is no softer love.
No halfway to be marked.

You are me. Deep.

I feel you now, and I always will.

There have been times,
     and more to come –
     that you have hurt me.
But I shan't love you less.

My centerpiece –
     my emotional core,
     is fully branded.

I now own,
     and I carry,
     the eternal scar of your love.

# Marry Me

For all that is,
      It's only you.
For all the right reasons,
      my heart has been scraped and sculpted, by you.
For all that I can muster,
      I want to see your face and kiss your forehead –
      now and forever.

Days together with you are brighter, fuller – complete.

When you are near, my emotions swirl.
      It is as if I were smoke in a gentle whirlwind.
      I become happily trapped in a magnetic dance.

You clutch me.
      You envelop my being.

With you, I will build a home,
      safe, with clean windows and lavish pillows.

On sunny days, I will tend to you,
      I will fetch blueberries, bread, and sweet butter.

When it rains or is thunderous,
      I will hold you –
      so close that the rains and the dark of the day can't
      hurt.

I love you.

Jump into the dizzying pool of my loving soul.
Stay with me forever.

Marry me.

## Two Souls

In the dark of the night,
    in quiet thought,
    I stare at a clear sky,
    and watch stars that trace boundless.

For now, using no more than simple math,
    the known universe of three-dimensions
    has four-billion-trillion stars,
    one trillion for each person on Earth.

Amid such mercurial numbers,
    two souls meet
    not in a trifle of fancy,
    but by a measure of purpose, and destiny.

# The Grace and Order of Eternity

I have decided there is another place.
It has grand white French doors, with crystalline glass, that
open to blue moons.

It is a warm place, which makes little sense.
For it is empty – best described as black.
But I am always cold, so warm is welcome.

Moons pass with the fleet of time.

In that present, I have my body of the past.
And more.
And more I have been.
It is seen or felt - at least to me.

People and all.
People around me – no, a part of me.
Family. Friends.
And not them. Their embodied presence – their thoughts.

Commingling spirits.

No surprise then. My body leaves me at times.
It doesn't matter.
It wasn't really there.

It is all something greater.
Stars and math speak, perhaps allude, to this truism.
All are more than my knowledge can embrace.

You and me, and all souls.
We are together.

I am touched by your faceless smile.
I am roused by your body - remembered.
Fetched, relived again – forever - are those times.

Kissed by the uniting divinity –
all is rarified and lashed as one.
Timeless wonderment and love.
We imbibe the grace and order of eternity.

# A Rose Upon the Wash

Tethered to none,
a lone rose blossom floated helplessly upon the wash.

Once, this lost rose was part of something grand, even
mighty.
Then, strong and stolid, it was anchored.
Healthy, it reached up and up,
growing high across the face of rugged-colored rocks.

Life can bid cruel taste.
The fingers of nature tarried with force.
With the glance of a falling stone, the rose was cut
completely, but perhaps not cleanly, from its parental stem.

The parting was real but deceptive.
At first, the rose looked fresh.
All petals clung intact.
Yet unseen, the close knot of the inner flower suffered
instantly.

The severed bloom could do little – but fall.
It was a slow and quiet drift through warm, wet air.
The meeting of a known, yet unknown companion -the
teaming sea.

More a kiss than a splash, the rose found the water's top.

Sunrays of the greater world lit a beautiful sky.
They touched and cradled the fractioned blossom.
Basking in the light, the rose became a part of nature's
beauty.
It caromed freely in chaotic, yet ordered, waters.

Nights affirmed this somber condition.
Stars and moons sparkled in the darkest star-speckled sky.

There was no solace for the rose.
To the rose, what once seemed the grandeur of vast
eternity, became a fearful place for a dying soul.

Cut off and alone, soft petals became colored, golden, then
browning.
It was the continued start, a turning to the new, to the
unknown.
Chased between the rocks and the shoreline's sea foam,
supple life became terminal and frail.

An existence whole and special had changed.
Isolation magnified, and the lone rose suffered.
Time ticked without reference, without structure, without
ties.
All passed empty in a saddened blur.

Hopeless for this world.
Trapped in wasting form.
There was no more to do than follow the Sun, now set for
others.

Bobbing and wasting in the wash, with time irrelevant,
the rose waited anxiously,
living a fading life –
unto death.

# Oxygen Is Finite

Days so many,
      each casually spilled to the next.
With mindless disregard, I simply breathed –
      ignorant that oxygen is finite.

An accident –
      so distant that in the hazy decades after,
      the lingering hurts seem all but lost.
I was still ignorant that oxygen is finite.

But,
      a runner I was.
      and still, I was caught –
      the prescription of death rang with reality.

My chest split open.
My heart stopped – purposefully.
Knives, cutting, blood, and belief – hope and ick.
I clung to minutes, hours – life.

Awoke.
I was there, in a freezing room –
      clatter, tubes, confusion, and pain.
I couldn't imagine the wretched path ahead.

Days passed.
Days, not so many.
I demanded – no, I coaxed fleshy parts.
I learned. I am less immortal than I thought.

Alive, invigorated while dragging my tatty shell.
Pains lessened – sometimes.
Good, or great, or just conscious.
I now know that oxygen is finite.

And that's ok.

27

# Placid Water

I stared at the placid water clear,
I saw your face, not mine,

Your heart and frame are miserably dear,
an artist's portrait is drawn so fine.

My eyes are tricked by a loving heart,
for mirrors never lie.

Cruel did come and tear us apart,
and one of us has seemed to die.

I miss you more than I can say,
I wish that you were here.

You're in my thoughts every day,
sometimes I shed a tear.

As chatty waters make their flow,
it's only you I miss.

When warm winds come and make their blow,
I imagine it's your kiss.

In time, the lake will mirror me,
I'll find myself again.

For now, my mind just cannot see -
a broken heart, your loving face,
and the vision that made us best.

# Angels

With the faint tremble of a dying moment,
        terror and sadness were wrestled to peace.
The lost compass finds a clear direction.
All is again bathed in light.

With near indifference, we tarry and dither -
        following our lives of normal cause.
Amid movement and calm, they are there - unseen,
        protecting our frail lifelines within the circle of the
        divine.

They clutch our arms and steady our quivering souls.
They breathe with fragrant breath and whisper in echoless
voices.
As we pass about this endless cosmos,
        they are our devoted guardians.

And we will chant:

*Thanks to you, oh angel fair.*
*I shall not cower by day or by night.*
*You have held me close in my despair,*
*And guided me from my dark and fright.*

# Arromanches–les-Bains

A sandy shore with mottled rocks.
Houses resting serenely atop calm cliffs.
Little waves offer a pleasant cadence,
twitching blues, greens, and yellows – from warm sunlight.

Air is enlivened by the distinctive notes of sea spray.
Faithful winds carry cool breezes.
All is fresh, alive, and sadly - pitifully - ironic,
this place is so tranquil - now.

Be slow to smile.
This is a tease, a deceptive bright face.
It is a mask covering a dark, eternal tragedy.
The skeleton of those past heroes - of souls lost.

True that waves roar ashore with freshness and lyric.
But it is their duality, as waters caress the hunky rusty tanks
below.
They are the metal coffins for loved ones – lives pinched
and snuffed in battle, lives of those acting to save us.
They are now dead – here - on Norman shores.

To preserve our known lives, world forces did mount.
All to win.
All to lose.
The might and mighty for a single June day - for D-Day.
Together, they stormed, bled, and cried.
They were upon five French beaches.
Strong men, mustering courage for us – their posterity.

Before the act, attrition was contemplated. It was known.
But prospective loss never measures actual loss.
All were present so our life would sustain.
Many survived and prevailed
Yet, lest we forget,
suffering and death gathered together –

a wretch upon the shore.

Now, pretty days sprawl in open view.
We could be tempted to forget the past, the lives, the losses,
the hearts that suffered, that stopped – there.
And the tragic companion sorrow at home.

Actions in duty – heroes.
The hallowed beaches at Arromanches–les-Bains.

# Do You Know?

I am in pain.
It is a wicked nag and
      it lives persistent –
      somewhere roundabouts my heart.

      And drugs don't help.

Juxtaposed – it is the fractures of love
      that press my body frame and
      it tears more holes –
      new holes - in my struggling soul.

      And it makes me feel weak.

I love you.
In my aloneness, I know I love you,
      but you are there,
      dreadfully far, and far away - from me.

      And it hurts.

Do you know? Do you care?
Would you hold my hand and kiss my temple?
Would you help me pound tent stakes and roast potatoes,
      or would you share opera glasses at Swan Lake?
Can I believe that you too quake with loving feelings?

      And my head spins.

You would know. I know you would know.
I know you would know because I have confided,
proclaimed –
      and proudly and pitifully and totally confessed –
      all my love to you.

      And I am empty for it.

When I did. When I did, I knew.
When I did, I knew you saw it all as more than a wailing
puddle of emotion.
You transformed my hope into reality because you said,
     and I saw it in your eyes, and I trust what you said,
     and I believed –
     that you loved me too.

     And my mind found air.

I am in pain – still.
For I know we are in love,
     but at this moment -
     we are not together.

     And my merriment is lost as misery courses my
veins.

# Painted Water

We are not as dust or gas,
Swirling over and about in constant chaos.
We are founded, in place,
Creating a canvas of shape and design.

At times, we are a glowing, perfect blend,
Delicate limbs that mingle with the strong and tall.
When mixed close with the light,
Our colors meld in graceful splendor.

Touching, feeling, sometimes grabbing,
We try to build, to foster working roots that can grow.
It becomes a place of family, and community,
A place in which one feels at home.

Reaching up, we see some are lean, tailored,
While others spill wide in careless tangles.
It is the differences that entertain,
And add texture to a flat grey dimension.

Down deep, in the dark hollows amid the rocks,
We secret away our hopes and fears, our inner selves.
The rich earth is scattered over that hardened shell,
An elegant beauty is revealed in jolly flowers.

Winds can blow, and their harshness is felt,
While some cool skies and some sunbeams are blocked.
There are those of strength and size that offer shelter,
Protection and tranquility tour our tiny world.

Upon a sheet of glassy water, life shows bright,
A picture framed in evident order.
A flawless sight, a sparkling presence,
All shining radiantly upon the painted water.

# Laugh Lines

I call yours laugh lines,
      since you are young and pretty,
      and you feel pretty – deservedly.

So too,
      because they have artsy elegance.
So too,
      because I choose to be kind.

I have them as well.
More than you.
Perhaps I have laughed harder.
Or maybe I am older.

I want to see your face, streaked with dark, deep lines –
furrows.

All those lines tracing your temples, cheeks,
      and surrounding your withering, colored eyes.

And then - when we will grin,
      it will be a matrix of swirly folds.

They will confirm the story of rich and aged lives.
The sacred truth will be shown most evident.

It will attest to our time
      and all our days,
      unto the last –

Together.

And always with love.

# Be Easy

*Slow down, be easy.*

An older man, my grandfather, said.
      How could he know,
      my colorful – stressful, unique life?
      It was certainly different and important.

Thoughtful and heartfelt.
A product of years, of grey hair, surgery,
      and a generally tired body.

But youth,
      and ignorance, told me otherwise.

I thought of the future – not endings.
I was a builder, hurrying to raise markers.

Life must be forever – here, on this Earth.

Now, my foolishness winces with age.
I am the grandfather, bragging about surgeries and a tired
frame.

And I tell my children – *slow down, be easy.*

# Drawn to the Past

Odd, that paling sun-dried red,
      that smooth tin where once was sanddab brown,
      that crisp and yellowing label,
      that primitive latch, which never worked well,
      that old dirt tucked in tiny cracks,
That these antiquities will live as treasures.

Preserve the timbers and mortice,
      the fieldstone walls beneath the barn,
      the floating streaks and bubbles in the glass,
      the worn wood floors tied with square nails,
      the carriage house, the smoke house, the home,
The brick and boards, and buildings themselves.

Imagine whose hand laid the hearth,
      whose son toted the mason's sand,
      whose feet walked the lot,
      whose back raised the roof,
      whose wealth was seen and status measured,
Whose life was lived within the village?

I live – drawn to the past.
I am humbled by that which was before –
      by elemental structures –
      stolid and noble.

Odd that many will survive me.

## Interlaced

I love us –
     woven together on a couch.
Your leg atop mine,
     a hand here, and a foot – an elegantly turned ankle.
Your calf washes over mine.

Hands together,
     fingers squeeze – rightly.

Touch, warmth, breath – your breathing,
     and my breathing.

Oh yes.

Hearts beat – syncopation -
     minds and words toss and tease – sensuality.

Our bodies are, in fact, interlaced.
A seeming attempt to vulcanize our persons
     further and completely -
     to be a soulful oneness.

# The Garden

Outside my home, where grass grew faint but weeds grew
great,
I turned, troubled, and tilled.
From a jumble of dirt and rock,
I raked and made a clean, welcoming – garden plot.

Set betwixt the road and my door,
I laid a path of irregular flagstones, flat.
First toiling little more than mud,
there was hope – new living things would come with effort
and care.

Nested right - in the angled crotch of the house,
this place seemed blank, unblessed, with little more than
trace sun.
From fragile plantings came tiny flowers – impatiens -
buried meek, trust a cheery pattern of pastels to emerge.

Suffered by storms and heat,
they survived the question, can they last?
But calmer breezes, and kinder rains,
nourished green leaves and tender roots.

Midst the hurry of the day,
I would step out, and feed their thirst.
When the ground was moist,
I would kneel down, and pluck the sturdy, ravenous weeds.

Their care, feeding, weeding,
and vigilant watering became my pleasure.
Once small and delicate, flowers grew firm, even bold,
pinks and purples of every shade.

Temporal, they passed - a life of not more than a few
months.

But their shape and color made me smile, and I was
pleased.
Drawn was my time, but I was smart,
for I knew, and I truly enjoyed those happy moments.

# What is Mine?

I am puzzled and woeful.

My home, a place I had built beside a lake, is warm and comfy.

Perhaps the home is too big, the windows too many, or the glass too clean, for one day, a bird flew into the glass.

In an instant, it was death.

The bird dropped motionless on my deck. Its head was badly contorted - telling someone who knows nothing of birds. Its neck had been broken.

It's a bird. It's just a bird. But I was troubled.

There are lots of birds. Though they are pretty, entertaining, and melodic, I have eaten birds. Yet, they live in my company.

They are all living a life of uniqueness.

It was a robin, a female. I studied it - well, I looked closely at it. I took a photo, memorializing its pathetic fate.

At the lake, animals die. Usually, a shovel and a quick toss facilitate a simple burial, the last of their terrestrial journey to eternal peace. But I could not do it this time.

Uncoffined, the bird lay in its sad, lifeless repose.

With conflicted emotion, I watched the body, knowing it was not going to move. But that wasn't quite true. After a couple of days, bugs and crawly things invaded my bird, gobbling I don't know what.

Soon, there was nothing more than connected feathers loosely wrapping a defined spine and skull. Ick.

And still, I did not gather the remains. I said a prayer and told myself to scatter the surviving bird parts at sea – or in the lake.

> Yet no, lifeless and broken, we had a connection. The funerary was deferred.

I let the carcass and feathers rest longer, flailing just a bit in the wind.

While no prayer at that time, I was feeling the coincidence of reverence and dismay as I considered my dead friend. Weirdly, I would not go on the deck. Plenty of clean wood - big, but I did not want to encroach on hallowed ground.

> From inside, I carried on this peculiar relationship for several weeks.

My petty madness may be arguable, though I do believe I am the interloper. I had gathered brick and timber, glass, and the attendant cleanser for glistening windows. My home intruded on the natural habitat, a place of birds, fish, and things that crawled in the dirt.

> But for my presence, my bird friend would be alive. I am the killer.

The disconcerting aspect of my mental scuffle was that I was probably right. Homes, roads, and people don't have to steal from nature. My primitive predecessors had constructed windows, once holes, covered with skins, and that evolved to wavy soda-glass and later produced fine panes of architectural excellence. These should not be the concerns of simple-minded birds.

It was true. My peace and pleasure came at the expense of my long-gone robin.

Was my mind simple and sober? Was I amplifying a sense of health and respect, or had I descended into some dark and bizarre emotional crevasse? Who is so moved by a dead bird, and who hallows such a death by watching a body decay? With cardboard and a broom, I finally scooped up my lakeside compatriot. With grace, I carried her tiny bones and crooked feathers down to the lake's edge. With a sad, but hopeful prayer, I scattered them in the wildflowers.

She was again amid his earthy home, and I found myself confused. What is mine?

The proposition was circular. It produced a modest haunting, but of course, I got over it - mostly. I continue to watch as a king – sitting stately from the balcony of my handsome manmade home. I still enjoy the water and all the creatures. Yet there is a tad more – I now value their presence more than I had before. And in certain moments, too many moments, I wonder.

What is theirs?

## You're Not Seven

By the Christian God,
came all that is –
in no more than seven.

Art redefined,
masterful impressionistic painters -
the great lot of seven.

Red, orange, yellow, green, blue, indigo, violet.
a spectral bliss –
a rainbow alive in seven.

But not you,
there is no seven -
surviving you will take a mercurial number.

Bathe my eyes in a mystic tincture
and they will still see you –
radiant, loving, and connected to me.

Through a teasing emotional mask
I will spy pearlescent eyes, high cheekbones, full lips,
and then wander to the rest of your frame.

We have kissed - a past,
enduring moments rekindled –
the perfume, the breath, and such.

Kisses came with arms and hands.
Bodies press
senses soar – very high.


You are not seven,
or twelve, or any near number -
you are grand, lasting, and beyond.

I am indelibly marked,
by your grace, by your kindness,
by my uncountable love – for you.

It is all my loss.

# Time

Healthy, my life moved with rhythm and break.
    A normal struggle and passage for me.

*What of the time that we could have shared?*

Aware, a little talk, and floating notes.
    No suggestion of more there could be.

*What of the time that we could have shared?*

Confused, as you were hard to read.
    Were you trying to come closer to me?

*What of the time that we could have shared?*

Gone, are days one can pointlessly count.
    A sad recantation of what might have been.

*What of the time that we could have shared?*

Easy, I can sink and weep for this past.
    Jumbo tears would well and drizzle over my skin.

*What of the time that we could have shared?*

Reflective, I know that none can be retrieved.
    No agony or forceful effort will allow such a win.

*What of the time that we could have shared?*

Here, you dance in my heart and on my hand.
    Things have evolved, a majestic plan to say.

*What of this time do we share?*

Warm, and together with you, I live my present day.

*I love my present day.*

47

## You Are Beautiful

If you did not live within the constructs
of divine proportion,
I would still find you attractive, pretty,
gorgeous, even breathtaking.

You are beautiful.

Does it take a Greek – Euclid?
Need I his work to tell me that you are lovely?

I do not.

Are we too rational?
In this world, we find words – the golden ratio
or the letter phi, to appraise beauty.

Numbers alone cannot judge beauty.

Must we live small-minded?
The human form, adaptation – the evolution
speaks to differing lines.

The universe is grand, and so are all its different
souls.

Is there a risk in measuring without depth and dimension?
Flat pages and photos are all measurable,
but they cheat the realities of curves and curvature.

My hands touch more than a page.

Should I align with the math?
Even if so, it will be but a small tell.
I will judge you by your mind, by your voice,
by the sparks in your eyes, by your smell,
your grace, your laugh, your empathy, and your emotion,
by how you see and measure me.

You are beautiful.

# In A Moment

The watery flow of time is effortless.
Rhythmic seconds become minutes, then hours.
Days march on and meld into lifetimes.

So too, our mortal existence passes
as we tarry about on our single Earth.
Foreseen or not, the final days approach, and change nears.

Wisdom, fatigue, encroachment,
our house, the fleshy shell, weakens.
Death reaches for our hand.

Sometimes, we remain quiet,
or perhaps loud, angry, sad - often tearful.
Our past is as clear as our future is unknown.

We will each meet this passage,
But each differently, for our views vary.
For us all, this time must come.

There is a period before - months, weeks, days,
when we are warm, impassioned, of feelings.
Then, in a moment, we are gone.

The quiet body falls motionless as the heartbeat is wrested
and the eyes empty with painless force.
The abundant soul begins a journey anew.

I've watched the final hours pass,
and until my time,
I will live on,
in amazement,
of that transitory instant that life leaves -
in a moment.

## Splash of Tears

The splash of tears need not yield the why.

Sad and sorrowful – from hurt and loss.

Happy and warm – cheering irrepressible joy.

Or both,

sometimes close together.

Oh my…

I will be present.

With care, I will collect your tears - good and bad.

I will consider my place in their birth - my need to evolve.

And I will do all I can to make your next tears

- Lovely.

# Tintagel

Against the rugged western coast rises massive -
an uncut, yet perfect, jewel.
Thrust high by the divine of millennia past,
this gift stands forth, a headland.
Alone, kinetic amid the violent water's wash,
the morphic sentinel looms tall, Tintagel.

Not quite an island, a hardened finger reaches,
it ties this place to all of England.
Early, whence man trampled the land by foot,
did this grand rock draw fancy?
Who of the ancients came there?
And they that did live, rested, and died there, upon
Tintagel.

Inhabitants from Rome, certainly those from the middle
years, even the fanciful of another - Arthur.
Born like the rock itself, of mystery,
of an origin ne'er to be known, or of pedigree precise.
Even now, does Merlin spook the tides?
In all the speaks of time, wicked and sweet,
it has become the legend of their home, Tintagel.

Pale the myth, this splendor is no secret.
Atop sheer cliffs, they built dwellings, basic, now old.
Primitive villages of survival, hope, and life.
Position, posture, and harnessed strength, they built a
castle.
Walk and walks, woven tight, fit to, and upon
that precious rock, nature's chosen Tintagel.

Play on in rhythm and rhyme, as waves fall
in aqueous harmonies, constant, lyrical.
White sea spray bathes this simmering garden, and it
blossoms - full - like an open rose, landed in charging
waters of lapis lazuli.

Looking, sharp slate glows softly as moist air forms a
spectral dance.
The rock is forever crowned, Tintagel.

Truly, this place does befit royalty.
Upon this planet - Earth -
there shan't be but a few places of such heroic form,
with such furry of sound, or romantic tale.

Be it known that upon an English shore,
looming mighty, from a virtuous perch,
is a timeless beauty, Tintagel.

## It Is the Kiss

It is the Kiss.

Perhaps not for lobsters or barnacles,
But for me – for me with you.

It is the kiss.

# The Waters of Hope and Calm

Cut, stitched, banged, and sometimes bleeding,
        I sit - alive.
By necessity, I sit too much, yet still, I sit.
Like my body, my mind suffers quietly;
        it plays a second to my physical bedlam.

My broken body has been pressed to move -
        recovering in a painful convalescence.
It is now my mind that feels shriveled
        from my old norm,
        seemingly slow, dusky, and dim.

I will have to find fiery pokers and sticks,
        clumsy objects that will not only punch,
        but force me to rekindle my mentality.
My wisdom and my craft are secreted somewhere -
        all buried, but not dead.

I must become the middle runner,
        the second, the third, or fourth in the relay -
        the one that moves from moment to motion,
Like them, I must spring forth, come to speed
        and move in stride with my surroundings,
        and secure the baton.

When I do, the seedlings, the misty ideas -
        those that troll in my head will gather, and fuse.
As the waters of hope and calm wash my mind,
I will discharge the clutter, sort the old and the new,
        and trap the errant and scattered thoughts.

Easily and unwittingly,
I will build and rebuild my cognitive soul.

Near glowing in new intellectual bliss,
I will become enabled and elevated.
The rebirth of my mind

will promote great happiness,
and return my grace.

## Words To Tell

Words, they live, beguiling, or errant, secreted.
Elusive are words that I want to surface.
At this moment - I want, I need, I implore
        my mind to dig, and dig again.
You are loved and must be told.


I want my words to have round edges.
Careful but carefree, and falling softly upon the ear –
your ear.
Reflective - I remember, I treasure
        the demand upon my soul to kick and feed the task.
You are loved and must be told.


From the lyrical phrase, there is cadence and tone.
Drizzle in the air, then sing and move.
Wishful - I tender, I hope, I offer
        my heart to you, to mold and torture.
You are loved and must be told.


Search for words gritty, melancholy, dark.
Contrast the words up-tempo to pop in the sunlight.
Encircled, I was, I am, I will be
        closing the loop to entrap our past.
You are loved and must be told.


Land my kisses - welcome, impassioned.
Savor those sounds, skin to skin.
Today - I think, I trust, I engage
        my toiling limbs to face ahead.
You are loved and must be told.
The words drift into me, clever, kind.
Relief as I offer a voice.

Empowered - I scratch, I whisper, I shout
       to lay down, cascade rich upon the page.
You are loved and must be told.


Weary of the task, troubling, humbling, rewarding.
Done, they live now and as echoes.
Take them - I give, I imagine, I burn
       for your touch, the sensuality of hands and such.
You are loved and must be told.

# The Keyhole

Crouched -

I look through the keyhole,
Lifeless, colorless, and hollow.
In private intrigue, I see so clearly,
Things different, the same, and some so dear.


Rules –

Never to see in a private place.
Only if harmless, so as not to disgrace.
A narrowed view as to expect.
Yet mostly unknown, so not to detect.


Empty -

A space is shrouded, and could lead to a blank,
Yet views are painted, and measured by rank.
A vista set nicely with logical frame,
Every scene is unique and warrants a name.


Curious -

Many are public and live not in locks,
But stand elegant and noble, within ancient rocks.
Though seemingly scarce, they do abound,
Anchored and lashed to long hardened ground.


Found -

Keyholes exist here and about,

Some on the horizon, some inside, some out.
Invisibly placed as another body part,
They tease our spirit and touch our heart.


Wonder -

What lies beyond each surrounding wall?
Is it mine to know, to care at all?
In nature, many keyholes loom to be,
Pretty and floating, like art on the sea.


Treasure -

A little glimpse of something, often greater,
Study them now, and again sometime later.
Surprise to for the vision that seems to be,
But offending no one, for what one would see.

## You Have Been Loved

In moonlight through the glass, there is a soft glow.

> You are at peace.
> I watch your chest, snoozing, not snoring,
> your easy rhythmic breath comes and goes.
> I study your pretty form.
> The waves of blond hair, long lashes,
> a fitting nose, a face inviting.
> I feel your warmth.

**It's 3:14, and you have been loved.**

The bathroom fan muffles your voice.

> You are cheery after a steamy shower.
> Toweled and dry, you are perfectly clad.
> Check your frock, pressed and smooth.
> There is a half-smile issued by you, and for you,
> the product of your lavish girly fluff -
> blush, mascara, eye shadow, and a splash of perfume.
> You own the look any woman would wish.

**It's 7:05, and you have been loved.**

Attentive - mostly, the meeting marches on.

> Work can be work if too tedious.
> An idea pitched by a monotonous voice,
> another genuinely clever concept, and talk continues.
> Sunlight bathes the room, pulling my thought to you,
> the jacquard on his tie, her airy silk dress,
> handsomely turned legs of the boardroom chairs.
> My toil is lightened for the associations.

**It's 10:33, and you have been loved.**

Lunch is a break, a wander away from the din,

    Time spent away to refresh anew.
    Among steak chewers and fish fanatics,
    I am a reverent salad eater at midday.
    The flossy restaurant has a garlic bias,
    the scent of scampi, and your favorite - scallops.
    I hear your voice in the upbeat lilt of the room.
    You add to the atmosphere and flavors.


**It's 12:27, and you have been loved.**

Day's end, but still a short moment for cards.

    Just a few hands before the dash to the train.
    Four men and a woman, but she's pretty tough -
    respected would be a better word.
    Only a few bucks in – so little time,
    Betting and bluffing. Hands play fast.
    They feign gags as I again praise you.
    In fact, they envy me.

**It's 4:32, and you have been loved.**

Home, amid the smells of an active kitchen.

> You fetch and fold.
> There is a clatter, a spoon to bowl, normal,
> you coax a recipe to combine.
> Dusting flour, an egg, a tad bit of lemon, curry,
> broccoli, firm red grapes,
> and cinnamon rolls with the sticky stuff.
> There is flour on your brow.


**It's 6:24, and you have been loved.**

I see you in the scant but sufficient light of the bedroom.

> You are all that you ever were.
> Is the excitement new, or has it been unending?
> You fill this place. You fill me.
> High cheekbones, soft eyes, shoulders, hips, legs,
> lace and buttons, motion and desire,
> hands, fingers, lips, and such.
> We are blissfully skin to skin.


**It's 10:48, and you have been loved.**

## Perfect Voice

I crave the sounds of measure and rhyme,
  to hear songs sung is always a choice.
Let harp strings play their watery tunes,
  each fitted with words and a perfect voice.


A sad life indeed if sounds not to be,
  a gift is given easy, to hear, and to play.
Early and late, an anytime friend,
  music aloud enriches my day.


How lucky they are with bodies so rare,
  their voices unique with the pitch hit right.
I clamor with others and cherish my seat,
  as they share their craft every special night.


Were the gift given more loosely than now,
  then it would be me possessing that sound.
But selfish not, I would always share,
  the notes, that treasure, with those all around.

# Gone and Again

Crumbly and scattered,
      ragged pebbles trace far back
      to a time so unknown to us now.
      Even these little stones must complete their evolution
      - to dust.
      Our ancient Earth is scarred and messy.


Gone is what was once purity.
      But look twice.
      Now is cut something neat, something so long at rest.


Gone and again


Dry seeds act like no more than death.
      Their rest is dribbled amongst the muck and worms.
      All dress atop plush soil within the furrow,
      a bedtime within that which was torn and hobbled.
      Tender - again, quiet in hope and trust.


Gone and again


Spark - the seed alive is again moving.
      Craving the light, the air, the watershed.
      No more the death mask.
      Contrast the pasty ground with green promise.
      No more than the another start.


Gone and again

Blue skies join clouds and spill their rain.
    The nested dirt chokes to mud.
    Too little, too much, perhaps enough.
    The furrow breaks against gnarled shoots.
    Strains persist for the Sun, for health, and the seeds'
present life.


Gone and again


West winds toughen – survival challenges.
    For some, faint slips in tickled plots vanish.
    Even so, some are of confident sturdiness.
    A tree trunk in spirit.
    A reality marks the bud to be reborn.


Gone and again


A stealth retreat relinquishes to a flower burst – again.
    With grace, they wave in unsung color.
    Maturity paints a cadence within a jolly day.
    Not so frail, all live courageously amid cool nights.
    Now fresh, a perfect thing – again.

Gone and again


And then, the terra life fades.
       Part of a lazy fall, sad petals let go as colors change.
       Hapless, they will dress the cold furrow.
       Proud, yet dismembered, there is the new await.
       Seeds relax in their seasonal dormancy.


Buckling Earth breeds texture and form.
       A great hothouse for living things.
       The place of fade and renewal.


It is that which is gone,
       and will be again

## The Candle

I will live vigilantly,

     Forwarded whole by effort and trust.

They will call me the Candle.

     For they will study the flame –

     First, believing it is a sad, flickering tear.

     But if they look again, they may smile.

     For the tear glows bright -

     Straining to warm each of their faces,

     And all that is about.

# For What You Said

I am adrift
    bobbing aimlessly in the emotional abyss of a
    pulsating sea.


Unconfined pain radiates from unwanted places,
    from my useless hand,
    from beneath my ribs and deep within my neck.


They are critical but pale to my loneliness,
    a condition that has a gross measure on a sad, ill-
    defined scale.


For what you said, I have felt you far when you were near.

For what you said, I have wrapped and secreted emotion, for
you, as my friend.

For what you said, I have puttered with things, wondering
and wanting you, a warm kinsman.


And then, with my bones broken, my muscles cut, and my
heart in shambles, you confessed -

    there is passion,
    an unuttered connection,
    new to me,
    old to you.
Unexpectedly,
    my life changed in spontaneous delight.
My mind danced within a dizzying fog of grateful hope.

For what you said, I have felt you far when you were near.


But I am here,
      still twisted and wrecked,
      all while you are there tailored and pressed.
So unlikely, even unhealthy,
I am the helpless fish twitching upon the deck.


My day, and yours, so you say,
      loses time to thought.
For me, it is of you.


Days have clattered on.
I find it easy to say -
I love you.
A confession to you or one to me,
      or the icing on a jumbled thought?


For what you said, I have wrapped and secreted emotion, for
you, as my friend.

It is the pain for where we are,
      apart for certain - perhaps for right.
It is odd, unwelcome, but inviting.


Treasured -
      yet troubled, for the touch, the lyric of your body and
      brow.
All are missing in this special mismatch.

A test?
A tribute to persistence?
An open idea yet to finish?
My noisy mind hears my soul walking alone.


For what you said, I have puttered with things, wondering,
but wanting you, a warm kinsman.


I love you,
       though my rickety frame fails to cradle my heart.
This may be folly and mayhem.


Do you truly love me?


Rest my channels of thought.
If you are a ghost,
I am lost all the more.

# Coaxing Dirt

More than dirt and grass, and wiggly worms,

I seeded ground that I had tilled and scattered with fish guts.

I hoped for spring rains, which did dapple the ground.

> I waited impatiently for the would-be gifts –
> the fitting reward for my dirty hands.

I am the amateur to those who follow a full life,

their souls instilled with a divine linkage to the land –
lassoed by rote or heredity.

Their view goes beyond the static plains.

They enjoy a satisfying home, a place of purpose that
demands food and promotes feeding.

> Their minds trust the roots to bear a promised
> harvest.

For them, farming is life, always tending with sweat and
prayers,

coaxing dirt, seed, and water to nurse a fledgling crop.

But some years, fickle nature plays cruel.

Damn the weather that lives within dark clouds, that
menaces,

and crackles with the careless violence of a torrid storm.

> Welcome is sunlight's blessed touch - kissing the
> face of each field.

In time, nature paints each plant its perfect color.

The seed and the farmer's joint dependency

produces a bounty to gather and share.

We will admire and thank those who have ties to the land.

> Each of them is noble and working toward growth -
> anew.

## Greek Goddess

I stared at you in your bedroom, dark but for candlelight, with music in the background.

> You sat thoughtlessly, looking back at me with a faint smile.
>
> An easily tied knot of finished ribbon struggled to capture your modesty and close the cream-colored silk nightgown draping from your shoulders.

Your hair, auburn blonde with soft waves, perfectly framed your face and drifted to your shoulders.

> Expressive, symmetric brows drove your beautiful brown eyes to mine.
>
> Unavoidably, your high cheekbones further beset your warm eyes. Broken only by defined lips, your small nose with a slight curl complimented your sculpted feminine chin. Trace light from the candles painted your soft silhouette on the wall.

My emotions rose, and every part of my body wanted to reach out and embrace you.

> Slowly and spontaneously, I smiled and said, "You look like a Greek Goddess."

> We both knew the comment was primitive and genuine, and that it came without a prior plan. Both of our eyes glossed as we sat watching each other before the night unfolded to other things.

The next day the honesty of those moments clawed at me --
in a good way. I decided that I would memorialize that
heartfelt time.

From a sheet of paper, I fashioned a card and wrote,
"You look like a Greek Goddess."

Fed fully by more than the moments of that night, our
friendship, romance, and love continued to grow.

A couple of years later, you reached into your coat pocket,
the emerald green coat that just covered your bottom and had
pockets sewn with white thread.

You pulled out a crumpled and torn piece of paper --
the Greek Goddess note.

Your face got caught in a happy struggle. Tearful,
you confessed that you carried it with you most days.

Fighting the rain some months later, you were again wearing
the green coat, and I asked about the note.

In seeming catastrophic conflict, you burst into tears,
saying it had somehow been lost.

That night, I sat down and reflected on all that you
are and how I truly loved you. I wrote you another
note that again read, "You look like a Greek
Goddess."

And at another time,

it landed in your hand.

74

# What Would the Kids Do?

A haunting, too persistent, and melancholy - a twinge.
Owned by me, it is a self-inflicted tease, a burden, or even a
pain.

Old memories – yes.
Some are dark, or at least not warm and bright.
But then, we all have these needling intangible issues of the
past.

No - this is the weight of things, of literal objects.
Large and small, they would clunk if dropped – some just a
little.

My unclean mindset whispers they must be kept – treasured.
But that is wrong, a crooked falsehood.
One I feel I must put right.

All this mushy thought has evolved with time.
I am not 15 or 20.
Pieces have become the abundance of rooms.
It is the proud sadness of living decades – of accumulating.

Pretty sometimes.
Valuable on occasion.
Meaningful – not as I might believe.

This is not an errant gene.
It is environmental. I was not born to save.

I was not.
I am not.
I will never be – a hoarder.
But there are still pretty bobbles on the mantle—things I do
not need.
John Hancock did not sign on my desk.
Things did not come over on the boat. I guess a few did.
Some have value, but I have money – at least enough.

It is my wiring, and my temptation to retain, that feeds my manufactured illness.

I am not that broken. Nor am I that petty.
It is an awareness that is tripping over the past, over this mass., blocks my future.
Seemingly quieted satisfaction is disquieted by my mental twists and turns –
by the time lost amid my stuff.

What would the kids do if I died?

# I Want You Here

I want you here – right now.

Looking at you,

I would dive deep into your eyes.
Naturally, my gaze would find your long flowing hair,
        your lips, and the dark brows framing your eyes.

I would move closer.
Quiet, I would reach behind your back,
        gather the blouse tucked just above your belt loops,
        and pull you close.

I would press lightly for a kiss.
Both our heads would have to tilt, just a bit, and then,
        the kiss would be slow, wanting to move to chaos,
        but waiting, and building.

It would be me who would loosen the first button of your
blouse, each of us in a seeming hurry.
With conscious restraint, I would move slowly.
Together, we would find ourselves properly and fully
undressed.
Breathing heavily, we would be close, and raw.

While you watch my eyes and laugh lines,
        I would push your hair back and cup your neck.
Again, and again - softly, I would kiss you as the prelude to
something more.
Unseen, blood races.

Chemically surging, I would move with repressed haste,
        failing to quell the excitement.
Succeeding in feeding the carnal romance.
There would be errant noise amid the sweet song of an
existing love.

Kisses and touch would share your body.
I would not be alone in this process.
I would want you to feel me, honest and complete.
Neither of us would be able to wait much longer.

And that moment would arrive,
        our bodies as one in a lyrical rhythm,
        with each finding their completeness.
It would be our most private and connected moment.
After, with you, aside from me,
        I would study and touch your lovely nakedness.
I would trouble your hair and smile.

I want you here.

## Scent

A life of all senses…

I could be placed,
  With hands still, at my side,
  With skin clothed, and warm,
  With eyes closed, even covered,
    Motionless, a place silent.

I could be teased, or tricked,
  Told I was inside my house,
  Told I was drifting at sea,
  Told I was lost in the desert,
    Off-balance, a place unfamiliar.

I would know better,
  From a sense of moisture in the air,
  From a sense of dust on carpets,
  From a sense of the held aroma of food,
    Unique, a noted persona.

I know this. It has a history,
  Of days spent in England.

# And There Are Sons

Jubilant - a father hears of a future, a new life.
        Anxious time lumbers until the grand day.
        And behold, it is a son.
A small promise of happiness, a treasure.

Whimpers and cries ring normal and welcome.
        There are bumps and turns of health and struggle.
        All parents worry and fear. But all pass.
A child grows, and so does hope.

Tender hugs, kisses, and wishes are imparted,
        From mother, from father, from friends –
        near and far.
        In time, an innocent face yields a smile.
The sparks of life, of growth. The passage continues.

Arms that once waived carelessly find strength and control.
        Cries once launched as vagaries become smoothed –
        purposeful.
        The world about comes of interest.
Extraordinary uniqueness becomes manifest.

Sounds heard are captured. A response is spoken.
        Steps are taken, cuts are found, and bleed – learning.
        Hours and days become weeks and years.
There are lessons in sadness and cheer.

Certain moments follow when the child rises high.
        Skills become powerful –
        the student dwarfs the teacher.
        Worries persist, but anticipation grows onward.
The evolution - infant to child, to adult.

For all that is the same, things change.
        The cradled hug becomes a handshake.
        A smile and a pat on the back affirm true affection.

Parting - though sad, speaks to the ability to return.

Sons verify fathers. They capture emotion and pride.
  Caring, even worry, lives on –
  trust and admiration unfold.
  A small soul rises to a man.
Mothers and fathers will forever love them.

# Among The Stars

You are before me, clothed and resplendent.
With and without a word,
my attuned senses fill with your grace –
      Sounds are harmonic voices, mutuality, and love.

Pleasant, oh so pleasant be.
These moments,
hanging crystalline, full, and free –
      Each poised happy upon the careless winds of our
      time.

Dance your cheery thoughts.
Smile your smiles,
sometimes tender, sometimes faint or falling –
      Chasing among the rushes of my mortal life.

Night, and it is dark and quiet.
I lay still,
thinking, my memory reveals a living record –
      As I look, behold your face, your touch, your voice.

I am here, and I am real.
Fractioned my person may be,
struggling, my soul pulls close –
      I feel your arms in my arms, my mind finds serenity.

The still turns to sleep.
Deeper is my thought,
dreaming, I fall into my peace –
      Circles close and my existence gains majesty.

From there, I reach out.
Senses glow as the body gains caress,
carefully colored is that life –
      Which I cherish, but is not quite my own.

In this place, mute are the conflicting noises.
Landed and budding cultures survive,
swept away are the dusty days of rules –
> Letting ancient origins live in harmony with the inner
> truth.

Take wing, join me.
Let your being soar,
find that place, we shall alight –
> To speak and hear the tempo of wispy songs.
Never forget my love.
Cast your eyes to the sky,
find my face in every sunset –
> And my heart among the stars.

# The Death

No Sun, no snow, no rain.
No necessary reason that this day differs, but
      all has changed, as:

      The world is now empty, by one.

Beset, before, back then.
But what seems like a moment ago, all
      was in balance, as:

      The world was complete, with each of us.

Loving conception, leading hand, looking ahead.
Loses when the voice of mortal life calls – back,
      to claim that tender shell as:

      The world returns a body to the dust, of one known
      place.

With care, with comfort, with concern.
With instinctive kindness, gather
      the kinsmen, the friends, and them all, begging:

      The world to share the pain and reflections of the
      person who passed.

Entrusted, enriched, encouraged.
Enveloped in the belief that life goes on – eternally,
      casting about glories of heaven, when:

      The world offers a unique soul, woven amid the
      divinity of all that is.

Tearful eyes, troubled hearts, tender emotions.
Suppressed sorrow for the existence ahead – happy,

in a trendy, churchy grandeur, the cosmic home
where spirits dance:

The world enlivens to play songs for infinity, echoes
for the universe.

Goodbye body, grace to you, go in peace.
Live anew beyond this terra globe, missed
        will be all we can think, when:

        The world enjoys the Sun that shines full, but you are
        not here.

# Can We Count?

Can we count the times I drove past your home?

> *... a whole bunch,*

> As I wondered, like a high schooler, what is she doing?

Can we count the phone calls that were peppered with laughter?

> *...lost owing to the great number,*

> But remembered as one great amalgam of a connected life.

Can we count your short skirts and fitted tops?

> *...a known number,*

> Looming large as a continuous and saucy seduction.

Can we count the times I have told you that you are beautiful?

> *....so many and more to come,*

> All honest and inspired by objective fact, and heightened by my loving view of you.

Can we count the feathers in our pillows?

> *...enough to enhance sense and sensation,*

A part of our chance to share our completion.

Can we count the times I flew away?

    *...noted and ticketed,*

Each caused me to miss you from the morning.

Can we count the times my heart has beaten since we were last together?

    *...millions and millions,*

We are never close enough.

Can we count the times I have told you I love you?

    *...it is impossible,*

Because I cannot stop.

# Peace

In drizzly platitudes, we talk and dream.

In voice, we say *we want* – peace.
We think of a grand paradise,
      an encompassing vista painted perfectly,
      and then we feel it could be genuine – peace.

Noble notions, we shan't condemn.

The heartened goal, we all want that – peace.
Come unto me - humble for the quiet,
      give us moments that ring true,
      and yet it seems so elusive – peace.

Find us that tranquility within simple walls.

Repel noises, stink, and fear to find a place – peace.
Let unlocked doors stand practical, not guarded,
      barring wind, water, and welcome seasons,
      and open our private hides – peace.

With touch, bind us to those dear.

Let passions grow, and love – peace.
Link our skin to topical sense,
      and hold us as limbs caress, imparting tenderness,
      and convey trust, all supporting – peace.

Envelop us full in watery harmony.

Bathe us as persons, our body whole – peace.
Pierce the shroud and through the crevasse,
      breathe in warm air, then fill fluid feelings,
      and let the spirit, the heart, let all bloom – peace.

# Bliss And Rightness

Far beyond.

A shriveling lone kernel
    in a full peck of corn.

They are moments.
    They are treasures,
    pinning themselves to my soul but 10 or 12 times in
    my life.

Upon arrival, they become infinite memories -
    of a time lived consciously, appreciative,
    and fresh.

Even more – Wonderfully.

These have been stunning blips in my fragile existence,
    no more than short, spotty events amid a raggedy
    lifetime.
    Born of the ordinary.
    Placed in precise measure, shredding my routine –
    that other me living commonplace,
    unseen,
    existing beyond control,
    fully detached from what we can
    call normal as to figure and form.

Unwelcome, but oh so welcome they have been.
    What began as random,
    and wandered about as a friendly apparition,
    grew and grew, building a blazing aura.
    Those soulful moments joined as the purity of life,
    cloaked with the emotion, occasionally of a romantic
    heart,
    a heart that might have been newly tethered to an
    attracted partner –

the other participant in that first shared kiss.

But mistake not.
    These rarities are far more than carnality.
    They are warm, occasionally rogue, heightened
    thoughts, emotions, senses,
    and they present across life's entirety.

Their presence lives internally,
    Masked to all about – except me.
    Warm and rising in rapture,
    a sweet overlay that arrived suddenly.
    Yet, sadly,
    the sensation lived short.
    All did leave with unwanted dispatch.

Devoid of chaos for experiences replete.
    The mind and body were encircled –
    fabulously and completely
    in the welcome toxicity of blooming satisfaction,
    of joy,
    and sometimes of love.

I was mesmerized.
    An invisible tell that emerged rhythmically –
    happily swirling and polluting the cracks and mushy
    ooze of my brain.
    With magnetic demand, it invited and required my
    body to be open,
    tending to my weakness,
    fostering the strength that pushed cascades of
    endorphins and other sweet chemicals –
    all filling the blank and longing crevices of a busy
    mind.

The greater good of this prizing bliss
    was the secreted nature of its beginning –
    the quacking growth of its gift,
    an inability to affirm control

and an absolute affection for the richness of its gentle
touch.
I wallowed drunk with a sense that ne'er a moment
will ever be as good again.

Kissed by this dance
        and close to tears with joy,
        it felt as if it was a thing –
        something to be controlled or channeled.

But no.

That will not be –
        for the grace of those moments was something born,
        even blessedly or conjured from within.
        All part of the perfect order that is ever-present –
        the grand and colored existence, deep in the infinite
        cosmos.

Majestic moments spring from cognitive embers,
        all helplessly aligning,
        and growing as curious mental whispers.
        They dawn unto us - engulf and enchant us,
        offering soundless but melodic voices
        that cradle me,
        gather my jubilation,
        clutch my dreams,
        surround my singular humanity,
        and find my truest love.

Measured good and great,
        these encompassing guardians of conscious life
        bestow that total calm, but it is always with caprice.
        For we knowingly and wittingly
        imbibe all of those cherished minutes,
        but they leave –
        stamping an imprint on our living spirit,
        yet teasing us as to when they will return again.

Stop.

Breathe.

Be empty.

I required this elucidation,
        the need to detail and promote
        the perfect moments,
        collected instances of bliss and rightness.

This past now surfaces bright.

For I was with you when one of these kindnesses -
        a rarity I have witnessed but a few times in my life,
        visited me,
        a gift sparked by your love.

# It Is Our Belonging

I see us.
We are close, so close your jeans brush with mine.
You are sitting on my right – better to hold you.

It is a rough and lifeless place.
Our feet dangle over a ledge, maybe a few yards above the ground.
It is neither warm nor cold, which is odd since we are on the Moon –
or some errant rock moving in space.
It is near enough to Earth that we can see blue – the blue ball.
In the darkness, distant stars are bright – I am able to see your face, but I don't know why.

I have three small brownie squares.
Each with a very thin layer of peanut butter frosting - one piece for each of us and one to share.
And I have several jumbo kiwi wedges with the skin trimmed off, though I usually eat it all - including the skin.
I have still water and green tea – you choose.

There is some atmosphere.
I feel minimal gravity – it tugs my arm as I hold you.
We see the flames of infrequent meteors descending – consumed in a fiery death.

It is quiet.
Yet not in an abnormal way – there is peace.

Your hair blows slightly.
But where does the breeze come from – I don't know.

I enjoy watching you.
It is especially fun – mostly because you like space stuff
And you are happy.
And I am happy – since you are happy.

You make me happy.
I kiss you.
Just a little, tiny tempting kisses.
That would be enough – at least for a moment.

You reach and hold my hand.
We talk about things – some simple, and others not.

It is our belonging.
And all because I love you completely.
I love you here,
and there –
now and forever.

# In My Life

You.

I want you.

And freedom – to live lean,
      loosely tethered, if at all,
      to relocate, live, relish, and love

You.

I want you.

And maps – to plat new digs,
      a home on a hill, or on water, or not at all,
      but still touched by flowers, a place cradling

You.

I want you.

And travel dates – to savor the world,
      even rocket to space, if all goes right,
      to sense something mysterious, that thrills and
      fascinates

You.

I want you.

And a view – the Mediterranean,
      waters lazily coloring the day if we're there,
      to charm the body to relax, and thoroughly comfort.

You.

I want you.

In my life now,
and forever.

# The Sentinels

In life
>  we move with thought and method,
>  or perhaps quick and careless,
>  without worry and too ignorant of risk.

Within our order
>  we sense guardsmen.
>  They are the sentinels,
>  standing close and far - to alert and protect.

At times
>  we see them and know
>  that they are there,
>  ever-present, helpful, and mighty.

In spirit and fact
>  they are fantastical,
>  caring as angels with soft feathered wings,
>  yet strong as warriors with sword and shield.

Throughout time they have stood noble
>  too often required
>  to live upon life's rough
>  and rocky shore.

Without their attendance
>  our small, frail frames
>  would be bruised, even broken,
>  but we survive for the courageous wreath of
>  the sentinels.

# The Beauty Within

Days should not pass.
    That you are not told
    Of your warmth and beauty.

All would say
    That God paid you fancy,
    For you are of a graceful form.

Yet seeing close
    There is more, not hidden,
    But beneath - in veil.

All things have that special within,
    In the cosmos or in rocks upon the creek bed,
    And within you - here, breathing the air.

In talk and touch, "tis found out as if secreted inside the rock,
    Beneath that fortress –
    Deep within the stone, the hardened shell.

An outer skin – a tease
    Maybe clean and attractive or rough, and bland,
    All teasing until cracked open.

Once split, there is the true self, and peering into the breach,
    We see - first confused in crystalline grey,
    Then emergent in a dusky haze.

Touched by the light of the Sun and Moon,
    Sparkles inside shimmer in a colorful glow,
    The reality - the majesty is shown.

And for you too. It is your kindly heart,
    Beating deep in a treasured soul,

That reveals you and your beauty within.

## Perfect Day

But once, unexpectedly drizzled in a few years span,

There grows the perfect day.

A bespeckled colored gem in God's great plan,

Made kind and right for children's play.

Comely winds do blow and dress the arid air.

Invisible wings carry singing notes soaring high.

Painted with a fragrance that floats without care,

All is ensconced within a deep blue sky.

Majestic and splendid, the magic we might call,

Be thankful for the active birth.

Rare days bestowed upon us all,

A memorial, a marker of our glorious Earth.

# Glistening Glass

In the darkest hour of the early morning.

In a quiet room with faint light beaming.

Cloaked by the shroud of protective walls,

I hear the chatter as raindrops splay,

> And I am safe beneath the crust of a sturdy roof.

Nakedly pure in emotional bliss.

Ever close, entwined, and embraced.

When bodies come to rest after passions play,

You drift faintly and perfectly to sleep,

> And I feel wildly close for our mutuality.

With the fragrance of English blooms just open.

With the warmth of embers still glowing.

On the nap of the soft woven carpet,

I stand at windows framed by billowing drapes,

> And I stare upon a storm through the glistening glass.

As droplets meld in blurry flows.

As spatters fuse in squirming waves.

When sheeting water runs crystal clear,

I watch dirt swirl in mud puddles below,

> And I see a new kingdom shining in the moonlight.

# Ardent Moon

Perched high in the bluing night.

Our friendly Moon rests with whimsy.

In a sky packed with stars, planets, and stuff,

This moon is never alone.


Likewise, though we spy from afar,

We too are connected.

Bright moonbeams reach out, touching us all,

They place soft, tender strokes upon our faces.


Not lost in a cloak of darkness, we belong.

We are lucky, for in the cool of night,

We are warmed in peace, and guided in unity,

By the ever-presence of our ardent Moon.

# Beside A River

There is a place where:
water, air, and the light of life
cradle so many of our tender souls.

There is a place where:
the divine has fashioned everyone
to rise upright and able.

There is a place where:
seeming infirmity is touched
with tenderness and love.

There is a place where:
special gifts are disguised
and hidden in a different human form.

There is a place where:
those blessed talents are revealed
in unique style and grace.

There is a place where:
the tempo, lyrics, and spirit
sizzles, and come to blaze.

There is a place where:
wrested patterns flow from
art's passion.

There is a place where:
pages are painted
with the hands of a loving heart.

Our place is beside a river where:
creative senses soar
in harmony,
with friends who care.

## A Time For Twin

A time comes when two become twinned.
An engagement is best without a hurdle or marker.
It is a time felt and saved,
when each hears the words of a silent voice.

Moved, the pulse quickens.
Instinctive passions warm.
Even a simple glance bestowed,
lands deep, far beyond the waiting eye.

There is no plea for sharing.
This shan't be for a begging phrase.
The desire is free and mutual,
as all are fused in connected truth.

Senses race beyond the skin.
It calls to life and inner-self.
Feelings arise as perfumed air carries
the wet breeze of another's breath.

Fanciful is an old word.
Nerves tingle as sensory evolves, sensual.
More than a raucous romp,
these souls are held in a close roundabout.

Kisses are shared, and limbs are entwined.
Gaiety entreats with each caress.
The mystic touch as bare breasts meet,
as willing mates delight in a quiver.

A dizzy world becomes mute,
Bodies sing in the raptured song.
Enveloped, this special place is private,
painted loosely in blazing color.

From a secret place is something given.
And completeness encircles them both.
As ecstasy fades to a wholesome glow,
the gift is real and will be forever treasured.

## Spaghetti Tubes

Theme parks, water parks, both inside and out,
For younger and older, they've grown all about.


An odd sight indeed, the wild spaghetti pipe,
Built for daring, speed, and sizzling hype.


Such technical marvels these guys have now made,
It tickles and thrills us, and that's why they're paid.


Built higher and stranger, and curvy, and such,
They thrill us and scare us, but not terribly much.


Go one, go two, try stunts like a clown,
There are no more choices; the ride's always down.


Now silly it is that a grown man would care,
But my children still query, will I go on a dare?


Nothing would be without water's flow,
To glaze the surface and hurry the go.

As we climb to the top for gravity's drop,
A lone path awaits us, but we cannot stop.


With shrieks and cries, the travelers fly,
With the sounds of horror, you'd think we might die.


The ride will end when the tube spits us out,
Let's go again, you'll hear us all shout.

# Castle

High and stolid does the castle stand,
a fearsome symbol to haunt all the land,

Watchful governance peering down from the sky.
Decrying to enemies not come nigh.

The mighty place to keep feudal swords,
a protective fortress for the grand noble lords.


Of rock and earth, the bastions rise,
to safeguard rooms, some filled with a prize.

See out around in the crosslet peer,
force prowling foes to not come near.

A watery moat built not for play,
but for guarding walls, keeping rogues at bay.


Through the barbican, one enters in,
to a fanciful village with much good and sin.

Quite odd the sense within those walls,
where merriment and torment do ring in the halls.

For some, a rare place they did come to see,
for some, it was home and their place to be.


But for thundering sword and fight of the foe,
the mighty keep rests quiet, in summer and snow.

When the waters dry and the moat turns to grass,
the chapel bells still ring for another night's mass.

Our frail human lives do perish so fast,

but the castle stands ageless and records its own past.


The fortress stands bold in such a grand place,
we forget the routine, the anguish, and daily grace.

On any day passing were kisses and tears,
only visible curtain walls can quench some fears.

Within the bailey, lives were lived and cried,
history cannot record all those who have died.


Resplendent today as when it was new,
the castle stands awesome in Earth's rocky hue,

Could they dream then how long it would be,
a noble protectorate for all to see.

The mortar and rock speak only to power,
its humanity recorded, within every tower.


The lives passed there, are now quiet at rest,
beyond venerable walls where they lived best.

The day is coming when we're not around,
and new buildings will land on now open ground.

But calmly and strongly demanding its space,
the castle stays founded, a bold timeless place.

# The Waters Of Humanity

In an earthen chalice carom dewdrops and raindrops,
all melding like a spring-fed pond.

It is a quiet, almost secret place,
common as many here and about.

A cheery crystal surface of the dominant blue
rests upon the prismatic order of nature's color.

From above the nested pools, water gently spills
over the lowest rise in the humble rock.

Quiet no more as shimmering waters rise in song,
a whisper becomes a chorus, divine, an anthem
playing on and on.

Ripples break as water dabbles into the lowest pool,
feeding a sparkling fingerling that winds out, and out
again.

Wind-washed flowers and trees are dusted,
rich and shiny for the humid mist of splatter and
splay.

The pastoral setting is completed with a vista of
greenery,    violets, and pinks, all traced by the light
of the setting sun.

This pristine place mimics the zest of life, visual and
lyric, a mosaic expressing the passions of the waters
of humanity.

# Hanoi – There, And Beyond

There, beyond the marker, beyond his marker.

       Beyond the sidewalk, over the metal rail.
       Not far, across the lagoon.
       Minimal now.
       Yet a hallowed spot – in mind.
       In some minds.
       Not in all minds.

       A hallowed spot
       Beneath the backdrop of new buildings.
       Meek under an umbrella of modern glass, and,

There, in that spot, loss, and worry – now past.

       Precise only in imagination.
       A painful point ill-defined, but known, a location,
       beyond the marker, beyond his marker.
       beyond the sidewalk, over the metal rail, and

There, hobbled and apart from his place,
       a man, a lone man –
       drifted down, fragile and frail, and unwelcome.
       Still alive, owing to God and courage,
       and the divine air, blown gracefully to his chute, and

There, beyond the marker, beyond his marker.
       Beyond the sidewalk, over the rail – splash.
       Long ago now – splash.

       An unwanted landing that became a sick treasure.

Here. Now.
       Before the marker I am warm,
       and I stand calm, unafraid,

yet my mind twists in a torturous game.

Here. Now.
     Before the marker, I reflect.
     With sorrowful imagination
     I picture, I hear, I see and smell, and I wonder.

     How could this have happened?

Those years ago.

     Years that are known to me.

     Years, from before the modern glass.
     In the darkness,
     In the water.
     In pain and screaming chaos, in reverence and prayer.

     If he had for a moment looked here, across the water.
     If he had dreamed -
     of the beyond,
     of another time,
     a later time,
     beyond the rail that splits the sidewalk from the water.

     Forward thought of a place - here - beyond,
     the would-be now, that is, a monument, and

There, in that spot, was not his end.
     For he was a gift of nobility, a man with a pedigree.,
     a warrior severed from his old home, from control,
     the pattern of life –
     all that had, all that would leave him, and

There in Hanoi, in the city - beyond the water,
     no more than a few blocks lived a prison,
     a wretched sanctuary for the feeble bones of war, and

There, in the blocks beyond, was cruelty, and shame –
    those jailors.

    Then enemies fulfilling terror:
    beaten bodies enduring more, and more, and

There, in dank rooms and tethered places, cells - cold,
    the beyond was that of displacement,
    of detachment and despair, hurt, of lost hope –
    for many.

    Fear, trust, and the sour breath of savage Earth, and

There, in the blocks just beyond,
    one can now walk, eat, laugh – a little,
    and ponder with safety.
    All those soft souls survived or perished.

And here, now, well-fed,
    calm with a coat, fitted shoes, socks, glasses,
    clean hair, and free movement -
    the reality that there is a door, an open door,
    the same door that was shut.

    A door here, not far, and

There, beyond the monument in Hanoi,
    a revisited place, the second dance in hell,
    a place marked forever in body, in mind, and

There, structured in the city of Hanoi,
    and implanted, and living unending
    in the minds of men,
    is a deserved monument,
    to the man among many men –

    McCain.

## Normal And Sweet

I come to you from behind.

I clutch you – gently. Or maybe a bit more.
Fingers, my fingers, cup the knobs of your hips.
There is a nascent tug. Is it from me or a little from
you?
This isn't about sex, or is it?

You like this. You have told me often.

I am close.

You are warm – normal, and sweet.
What you smell of, I know.

And things go on.
Or perhaps not. Perhaps I walk away.

In every case,
you have been loved.

## A Graduation

Educated, enriched, emboldened.
A goal has been reached.
Pomp and paper will mark the day,
But wisdom and compassion are the true measures.

Just a few days back,
He was a child - helpless and new.
Living life's quickened pace,
Days, months, and years have all rushed past.

I know this person. I love this person.
I am impressed with his years of growth.
From nothing sprouted primitive edges.
Those have now become soft and round.

It is only the beginning.
Ahead is a long journey, winding, exciting – and
pitted with hurt.
Healthy growth must find a harmonic pace.
Then, the presence of life can truly be savored.

So many great treasures are unseen:
Trust, peace, friendship, and love.
A grand pile of bobbles has little value,
if they exist without connected feelings.

For him, graduation is a passage, an earned
celebration.
For me, I yearn for history.
I will hope that he is never too far,
I would miss his bright smile on my face.

# Water Veils

'Neath careless sky and bending tree,
Rises vaunting spire of Salisbury.

A presence strong in century's Sun,
Greet the prayers and pains of everyone.

Stood I, quiet in grass and green,
All senses sop the passive scene.

I am so small, like a fallen twig,
Watching waters dance their swirling jig.

This is as it was in decades past,
A cloistered refuge in a land so vast.

Hear my dreams upon the river shore,
Trust I, that time will give me more.

That moment made by time then caught,
Will live forever in heartfelt thought.

Thanks that I did find this place,
Where lazy branches hang like regal lace.

Bright rays touch leaves with gold and white,
And they do glow like falling light.

In pristine elegance, the humble soul sails,
Where willows weep, like water veils.

# Special Person

'Tis rare that a woman can twine
charm, grace, gentility, and wisdom.
Yet, for one, the heart and the mind speak
Thoughtfully, in an effortless lyric.

For many years, warm words have been felt soft,
like the gentle caress on a child's brow.
Ne'er are these platitudes, but true voice,
carrying moments to completion.

She lives not of the I, but instead, of the "we."
It is the way she acts with many
that adds so much to her life, to all of ours.

This friend to many, is not a chatterbox,
but a kind heart, who sees the light within.
And this light bursts out
as she reminds us of our special place,
our home, with us, within us, within the cosmos.

Seldom do we frown, for she voices again and again,
"We are survivors," and so we are.
While the loose ends of life have sometimes hurt,
there is ultimately order, and her vision is right.

Son and grandsons are constantly moving,
stretching for time, in little scrapes.
They are like all beings.
She tirelessly cheers us on.
The family is always in her life.

I am so lucky, for she is my mom.
It is her hand that touches my brow.
It is her voice that enriches my thoughts.
It is her effort that adds to my day,

And I will always love her.

# Punting The Cam

Quiet eddies split from the bow of a blunted boat.
Beneath the Bridge of Sighs, a dank breeze is about.
Not Venice, but floating atop the English Cam,
we steer our punt on summertime waters.

So clever - the river, the schools, the time,
So pleasant - the friends, the day, and our awkward
vessel.

Watching,
we laugh as novice tourists slip and twist.
And for that, the boats turn here and there.
But the Cam is our river, and these are our schools
and books.
We know the skills and joys of the punt.

Young girls sit,
cast back like grand dames without care.
Upon the flatted form at the boat's stern, my feet are
still.
I know the movement, and I find my easy balance.

In shallow water, the wooden pole slides quickly to
the bottom.
But the pole must be pressed, and fluid physics must
offset the press, the pole. We travel straight.
With a learned stroke, the boat glides in grace.

A day framed by the Sun, wavy grasses, and college
bridges - the ancient stones of old schools.
We are together, resting within our play.
Time is well-wasted, punting the Cam.

## And Love

I stare through the midday sun -
to the horizon at the water's end.
Each faint wave feathered in azure blue,
all fit neatly against a near windless sky.

I spy sturdy blanched white sailboats,
straining to catch the heartless breeze.
Seagulls bobble in the waves' crotch.
Majestic cranes glide above the shoreline.

Green leaves beyond the sand dance on looming
trees, carving patterns in a rousing magenta sky.
Errant rocks, birds, and greenery form graceful
mosaics, marking in my mind,
the toil and play of life.

This day, and any such day,
I could call it perfect, and grand.
I savor this time and rue another path.
I should cherish it now – here, for me.

But no - this nirvana lives sadly for me,
I am here alone, accompanied only in the heart by the
thought - of you.
I see more - clouds, colors, and still more movement,
It is no more than a hollow clanging, reminding me
of when you were near - to me.

Life is living in dribbles and ripples, and places
squirreled away in tiny crevices,
a pulsing vista, warm and cold, pushing life forth,
To me, it lives pallid, faded by my grief, and
measured by the chasm in my heart.
I feel the hot Sun cold. The full day is empty.
It is your light, breathed to me in your eyes,
kissed to me by your smile, held to me by your frame.

All kindled by heart songs, your soul - so special that
it remains, a halo, encircling my every thought,
my every moment, all these days.

I am trapped in the wide open, in this flawless place,
centered in this welcoming chatter and din.
But I am worse than alone.
For I dally atop withering hope,
in a melancholy daze,
I die a little.
I wish.
In love, I long for all that we once were.

## In Their Eyes

Click – a photo, this place, a time,
a memorial, a textured screen.
See more, deeply, piercing,
consume the detail otherwise unseen.

Eyes rested, and those tired
have spied the herein sight.
So disciplined their labor,
so true, all lines set right.

Just days, weeks, or years ago,
places distinguished or rife.
They struggle to clearly see,
to show us the greater life.

Manet and Monet, or of the seven,
each saw the very same place.
With their hands, they dabbled with colors and lines.
They painted the very same face.

Enriched, a lingering feeling,
my thought and vision, does try.
They captured an eternal view,
set in my mind, and in their eye.

## Prelude

Awake – stars now asleep,

birds and twitters enliven a dull, but healthy, haze.

Tranquil thoughts shift – normally,

Crowded becomes my mind, of you, of all things of you.

And the day,

a growing, evolving, mosaic.

Egos and tugs – even some hurt,

The shoots and rooster tails, the accompaniment of life.

And you are there.

You are here – with me, within me.

Noon sun peaks,

Afternoon and evening come.

Not today; you are there, and I am here.

Curse the distance – apart – our bodies.

Always together in mind.

Soulful soulmates.

I want us – the glance, the gaze,

The sultry color of your eyes, the iris, all of the fine line details.

And kisses – little smooches, then big and bending,

just honey bunny, a trickle of all the more.

Sight.

The necessity.

Touch,

The more of sight and the more kisses.

The more thought and my waking day pondering – you.

I want to make you naked.

You are lovely, and it needs to be mutual, and private,

and sensually mammoth, and toxically great.

Much as the rest of the day,

it is a prelude.

## Small Hands

There are a few rare years,
when small, fresh hands, reach - up.
Soft skin, and little fingers
seem almost lost within the stable
grasp of a large, sometimes calloused, hand.

Moved, the child's inner sense
and desire seeks help, and direction.
This sweet, unwitting response, grants the title,
of leader, protector, and trusted one.

Often without words, these moments
are offered and accepted, simply, naturally.
It is again that we relate, through touch,
a part of humanity, directed, with purpose.

But little fingers grow,
and the child matures, confident.
Known not to them, this new loss,
for through little fingers, flowed up,
innocence, tenderness, and love.

Respective, I shall look back.
Forever crystalline is the view,
are the sounds, the smells,
and the faint breeze.
Always remembered will be that day – the last,
when unto me, a small fresh hand did reach - up.

## The Sum of My Regrets

Unsaid
Unfinished
Unknown what could have been

# Tommy Toucan Timothy Tuck

Tommy Toucan Timothy Tuck

built a little dump truck.

He drove it around.

and went bump, bump, bump,

and then it was ready

for the dump.


Second Grade
…surprised I knew the word toucan

Made in the USA
Las Vegas, NV
08 April 2024

88414303R10075